W9-AXH-303

The Berenstain Bears
and the
TROUBLE WITH GROWNUPS

Grownups and cubs
get quite a surprise
when they see themselves
through the others' eyes.

A First Time Book®

The Berenstain Bears
and the
TROUBLE WITH GROWNUPS

Stan & Jan Berenstain

Random House 🏠 New York

Copyright © 1992 by Berenstains, Inc. All rights reserved under International and Pan-American Copyright Conventions. Published in the United States by Random House, Inc., New York, and simultaneously in Canada by Random House of Canada Limited, Toronto.

Library of Congress Cataloging-in-Publication Data:
Berenstain, Stan.   The Berenstain bears and the trouble with grownups / Stan & Jan Berenstain.   p.   cm. — (A first time book)   SUMMARY: The squabbling in the Bear household between parents and cubs subsides after Mama and Papa Bear and Brother and Sister Bear perform humorous role-playing skits.   ISBN 0-679-83000-6 (pbk.) — ISBN 0-679-93000-0 (lib. bdg.)   [1. Parent and child—Fiction.   2. Role playing—Fiction.   3. Bears—Fiction.]   I. Berenstain, Jan.   II. Title.   III. Series: Berenstain, Stan.   First time books.   PZ7.B4483Bekt   1992   [E]—dc20   91-27430

Manufactured in the United States of America   13   14   15   16   17   18   19

Even though it was bright and clear outside
the Bear family's tree house, there was a
storm brewing inside. For while it would be
wrong to say that cubs and grownups are
natural enemies, it would be fair to say that
cubs and grownups sometimes don't get along.

"Where's the rest of my paper?" thundered an angry Papa Bear, storming into the living room. It didn't take him long to find Brother Bear and the sports section.

"I just borrowed it," said Brother. Papa snatched it up and plumped down in his easy chair. Brother wandered into the kitchen looking for sympathy from Mama Bear. "Gee," he said, "what's eating him?"

"Your father looks forward to his evening paper," Mama said, "and he has a perfect right to be annoyed when half of it is missing—and furthermore, I'll thank you not to refer to your father as *him*!" She stomped out of the kitchen.

"Why not? He's a *him*, isn't he? Gosh," said Brother, "what's eating *her*?"

What was "eating" Mama was Sister Bear. Sister had been on the phone with Lizzy Bruin for almost an hour.

"But Mama!" she protested when she was told to say good-bye.

"Don't 'But Mama' me!" said Mama Bear. "This is not your private phone. You've had all day to talk to Lizzy at school, and you'll have all day to talk to her tomorrow. *So hang up that phone now!*"

Sister did as she was told.

Later, at dinner, Brother and Sister got into a little more trouble. "Peas and mashed potatoes again," said Brother under his breath.

"And what," Papa asked, "is wrong with peas and mashed potatoes?"

Brother was about to answer that they'd had them three days in a row, but he thought better of it.

Instead, he began counting and spearing peas onto his fork, "One—two—three—four..."

"What are you doing?" asked Sis.

"Trying to see how many peas I can get onto my fork at one time," he answered.

While Brother was counting peas, Sister was working on her mashed potatoes. She patted them into a little mountain, and then using her spoon, she pressed a cup in the top. "Pour it right there," she said when Mama offered her gravy.

"What in the world?" commented Mama.

"Well, you see," said Sister, "it's a volcano, and the gravy is going to be the lava and flow down the sides."

"That will be quite enough of volcanoes and counting peas!" shouted Mama. "Food is to eat, not to play with!"

"Gee whiz," said Brother. "We're just trying to make it interesting."

"Food isn't supposed to be interesting!" roared Papa. "It's supposed to be food!"

Brother and Sister went to bed that night and got up the next morning without much fuss. But trouble started again at breakfast.

"Oh yes," Brother said, suddenly remembering something. "We'll be getting the late bus home this afternoon because—"

"Late bus?" interrupted Mama. "I was planning on our visiting Gran after school."

"But Mama," he protested, "we're staying late to plan for the Parents Night Talent Show next Friday."

"Parents Night?" she said. "First I heard of it."

"And Friday is my chess night with Farmer Ben," complained Papa.

"Here's a notice I brought home," said Sis, digging into her bag. "I forgot to give it to you."

"Me too," muttered Brother.

"Why, this notice is a week old!" said Mama.

"Forgot? Forgot?" roared Papa. "Why, you cubs would forget your heads if they weren't attached to your shoulders!"

"Phew!" breathed Brother as he fell into the seat beside Cousin Fred on the school bus.

"Tough morning?" asked Fred.

"You better believe it!" said Sister, taking the seat Lizzy had saved for her.

The four compared notes on the way to school. The cubs agreed that while there was no doubt that their parents loved them, they were a little difficult to get along with sometimes. They nagged; they said *no* a lot; and they never wanted cubs to have any fun.

"Hey," said Brother as they got off the bus, "what are we going to do for the Parents Night Talent Show?"

"Don't know," said Lizzy. "Let's think about it."

That afternoon the auditorium was filled with cubs getting ready for the show. Babs Bruno was playing her violin. Queenie McBear was practicing pirouettes. Too-Tall and his gang were working on a rap number, which Teacher Bob didn't look too happy about. Brother, Sis, Fred, and Lizzy didn't have an idea yet.

But as they searched their brains, Brother snapped his fingers and said, "I've got it! Remember what we were talking about on the bus this morning?"

"Sure," said Fred. "We were saying how grownups can be a big pain."

"Well," said Brother, "let's put on a play about that, and call it..."

"*The Trouble with Grownups!*" shouted all the others. "Sensational!" said Sister as they slapped hands, delighted with the idea of showing parents how hard it is being a cub.

But putting on a play is easier
said than done. You have to write
it, figure out who is going to play the parts,
then memorize it. Then you have to worry
about costumes and scenery. The cubs did all
that. It was hard, but it was fun, and they
did it all in secret. Costumes for Fred and
Lizzy were easy. They were going to be Brother
and Sister, so they just borrowed their extra
clothes. Getting costumes for Brother and
Sister wasn't so simple, because they would be
playing their own mama and papa.

They managed by letting Gran in on the secret.
She was a wizard on the sewing machine, and she
made them great-looking little Mama and
Papa costumes. The four practiced
their parts, and before they knew it,
it was time for the big Parents
Night Talent Show.

There was a lot of talent at the Bear Country School, and all the acts did pretty well, but it was Brother, Sister, Fred, and Lizzy's play that was the hit of the show.

The audience of parents laughed and laughed when they saw how they seemed to their cubs. Mama laughed until tears rolled down her cheeks. Papa laughed, too, but not as much as Mama.

They both thought the play, which was a big surprise to them, was very well done. They admitted that it helped them understand what it was like being a cub.

The next morning Mama and Papa had a bit of
a surprise for their cubs. You might even say
a shock.

Mama, who was a sewing wizard herself, had made a grownup-size pink jumper. Wearing it, she looked like a huge Sister Bear. She even had a pink bow. Papa, wearing a red pajama top and blue bottoms, looked like a gigantic Brother Bear. The cubs were confused.

"It's very simple," explained Mama. "You helped us understand what it's like being cubs. By pretending we're the cubs and you're the grownups, we're going to show you what it's like being parents."

Before Brother and Sister could say a word,
Mama and Papa began acting like cubs.

"Where's breakfast? I'm hungry!" shouted Papa.

"I hope we're not having that gooey oatmeal
again!" screamed Mama.

"Ooey gooey oatmeal! Ooey gooey oatmeal!"
shouted Papa, jumping up and down.

Brother pulled Sister into the living room, where they could hear themselves talk. But the living room was another shock. There were things all over the floor. Not toys, which they sometimes left lying about, but strange things like the vacuum cleaner, Mama's sewing basket, Papa's chain saw, and his wrench set. What a mess!

The cubs understood. Mama and Papa were showing them what it was like having to pick up after them. Mama and Papa ran through the mess and headed for the front door. Brother cried, "Please don't bang the..."

But it was too late. Papa banged the door so hard it shook the house.

Brother began to smile. Sister began
to giggle. They went out on the stoop.
There were "cubs" Mama and Papa sporting
about on the lawn—Mama jumping rope,
Papa trying kick turns
on Brother's skateboard.

But their feet got
tangled, and they
sprawled head over
heels on the grass.
Pretty soon they were
all laughing so hard
their sides ached.

Later, when they were back to being themselves, Papa said, "I have a better idea how cubs feel now." Mama agreed. Brother and Sister admitted they had a better idea how parents feel, too. "Boy!" said Brother. "You two sure know how to act like cubs!"

"After all, we were cubs once ourselves," said Mama. "And here's a thought: You'll be grownups someday and each probably have cubs of your own."

Brother and Sister thought about that for a moment. They looked at each other. Then they looked off into the distance and thought about it. It was something to think about.